Celtic Crossing

Celtic Crossing

By DC Fidler

DCFidler Publishing
2018

Published by DCFidler Publishing
1117 University Avenue, #505
Morgantown, WV 26505
DCFidlerpublishing@gmail.com

Printed in the United States of America
by Lulu Press, Inc.

ISBN: 978-0-9989729-5-4
Library of Congress Control Number: 2018901992

Setting

A modestly furnished living room with an off-set dining room area which has a door to the kitchen. There are stairs to the second floor. The house is in Brooklyn, NY. The play takes place from 1886 back to 1883. The house belongs to Harold Cullen. The scenes are told backward in time. In the first scene in 1886, a simple single bed has been moved down to the living room, since Harold can no longer climb steps. The house has electric lights until the last scenes in 1883 when the house is lighted by candles only.

Characters

Andrew Carson Cullen	Irish male, mid 20s
Harold Rupert Cullen	Irish male, mid 50s
Robert Scott Cullen	Irish male, late 20s
Eleanor Fianna Walsh	Irish female, late 20s
Elizabeth Sarah Walsh	Irish female, early 20s

Appreciation

Thank you to Travis Teffner for working with me to create a beginning story and to Sandi Constantino-Thompson who proofed my later drafts and diligently worked to guide me with her wonderfully helpful comments and encouragement.

Note

In contrast to formal scripts for use in rehearsals, this is a book of the script, containing more stage directions to aid readers to envision what can be happening upon the stage. Most actors prefer few or no directions, allowing them to discover and create the lives of their characters.

1. Harold's Living Room with Bed
Evening – 1886

*Soft, simple music begins in the dark. A spotlight rises on
ANDREW as the remainder of the stage remains in black.
ANDREW wears a hat and sweater and sits on a small
footstool near the front of the stage.*

ANDREW: Tonight, like other nights this month, I visit my
    father's house. I sit here on his footstool amidst his
    books and assorted fragments of art. The last month of
    Father's life, this living room served as his bedroom.
    Each night I come here and have a ritual of thought.
    My mind reviews what happened one month ago and
    from that moment works back in time.

*(HAROLD yells out from the dark and suddenly the
room fills with light from both electric lights and
sunlight coming through the windows. The music
ends. HAROLD is lying in a single bed in the middle of
the room.)*

HAROLD: No! On the end table!
ANDREW: Ah yes.
    *(ANDREW stands and pulls off his hat and sweater as
    to look dressed on a different day. He steps into the
    rest of the room, walking to a table with several books.
    He holds up one book.)*

ANDREW: And this top book is for Miss Wilshire?
HAROLD: And the one beneath it.

(ANDREW picks up the second book.)

ANDREW: This book? Rather tattered, don't you think?

HAROLD: Jonathan Swift. It belonged to a Miss Lucy ... Miss Lucy uh ...

(ANDREW looks inside the book's cover.)

ANDREW: Thornberry.

HAROLD: Miss Lucy Thornberry. A nanny on 5th Avenue. Her charge was kicked in the head by a carriage horse. She read one specific poem to the boy every night. Every night the boy went to sleep clutching the book, rubbing its spine with his thumbs in the rhythm of the poem. Thirty-two years she put him to sleep with that book. Thirty-two years the man-boy thumbed and wore that book's spine raw.

ANDREW: I see that. Two books of Swift for Miss Wilshire.

HAROLD: I read aloud from that same book to Miss Wilshire.

ANDREW: To Miss Wilshire? You did not.

HAROLD: Irish poems I did.

ANDREW: You read Jonathan Swift poems aloud to Miss Wilshire?

HAROLD: Recited.

(HAROLD points at his own temple.)

ANDREW: You did not.

HAROLD: Most certainly did.

ANDREW: Where?

HAROLD: *New Trinity Fleet Street Pen and Book Shoppe.*

ANDREW: Old Miss Wilshire visited your shop and you recited Swift?

HAROLD: She was young when we began.

ANDREW: In front of people?

HAROLD: In private.

ANDREW: How does one manage privacy in a public book shop?

HAROLD: Wednesdays. Closed for inventory.

ANDREW: Good Lord, Da.

HAROLD: Nothing carnal. Jonathan Swift poems.

ANDREW: I did not know our Irish Mr. Swift composed poems. Very well.
(Writes on his list as he speaks.)
"Two books of Jonathan Swift non-carnal poems go to Miss ... Miss ..."

HAROLD: Charlene.

ANDREW: Miss Charlene Wilshire. You are full of surprises.

HAROLD: You should recite Swift to Sarah.

ANDREW: I have not committed one line of Swift to memory.

HAROLD: I read Jonathan Swift to you when you were a lad.

ANDREW: *Gulliver's Travels.* Not poems.

HAROLD: Recite some other Irish poems.

ANDREW: Poetry doesn't glue to my brain, besides ...

HAROLD: *(Mumbles.)* Numbers.

ANDREW: What was that?

HAROLD: *(Loudly.)* Numbers.

ANDREW: Yes, numbers do glue to my brain, but as I began to say, Sarah is away visiting Eleanor in Baltimore.
(Mumbles.)
For an extended period of time I imagine.

HAROLD: Then bloody well don't recite a poem to her. When she returns *read* a poem to her.

ANDREW: Sarah would laugh.

HAROLD: Laugh?

ANDREW: Laugh at me.

HAROLD: Sharing classics aloud together is—

ANDREW: Yes, yes, yes. "Tis better than sharing a bed together."

HAROLD: Ah. My phrases glue to yer brain.

ANDREW: *(Mumbles.)* It cannot be helped.

HAROLD: What was that?

ANDREW: Your words clearly imprint in my head. Driven in with the subtlety of railroad spikes.

HAROLD: A father wants to pass along some blasted thing of worth. You will pass along the same words to this lad you will soon rear.

ANDREW: Sarah believes it will be a daughter.

HAROLD: It will be a son.

ANDREW: Oh you know this, do you?

HAROLD: Knowing the sex. A gift passed down to me from my father, and his father's father.

ANDREW: A son.

HAROLD: Oh ... oh.

ANDREW: What is the matter?

HAROLD: I am about to shit out my brains.

ANDREW: This minute?

HAROLD: Of course this minute. Tell Shirley to hurry in.

ANDREW: You ordered Shirley to take the day off.

HAROLD: Day off?! She is my nurse. My nurse does not take a bloody day off.

ANDREW: Remember Da? You demanded she not be here today.

HAROLD: What?! ... Oh. Fine then. Fine.

(ANDREW is silent for a long moment. This angers HAROLD.)

HAROLD: Then get on with it for bloody sake! Why wait for me to soil myself?

ANDREW: I am doubtful.

HAROLD: Andrew!

ANDREW: How can you be so accepting?
HAROLD: I made my peace.

(ANDREW is silent for another long moment.)

HAROLD: Andrew Carson Cullen! You placed your hand on your mother's grave and swore to me.
ANDREW: That I did. First? I brought something for you.
HAROLD: For me? I cannot see. What is it?
ANDREW: A wee something for your taste buds.

(ANDREW pours whiskey from a bottle into a glass and gives it to HAROLD.)

HAROLD: My taste buds are ancient. Your drink better be stoneyhearted strong.
ANDREW: It tis.

(HAROLD smells the glass of whiskey.)

HAROLD: Ah. Whiskey.
ANDREW: Irish. Taste it.

(HAROLD sips the whiskey.)

HAROLD: Kilbeggan?
ANDREW: Aye it tis.
HAROLD: What da ya know? A pint from my youth. We called this "pot still" back in my day.

(HAROLD drinks more whiskey as ANDREW walks to the desk and brings back a canister tied in a cloth. He unties the cloth, opens the canister, pours liquid onto the cloth, and sets the cloth on the foot of bed. He closes the canister and then walks to the couch and

gets a small pillow and returns to HAROLD. He picks up the cloth. HAROLD finishes his drink.)

HAROLD: Ah. "It lighteneth the mind."
   (Notices ANDREW.)
   Wait! Draw the drapes. I want it dark.
ANDREW: I know. I know.

(ANDREW sets down the cloth and pillow and closes the drapes.)

HAROLD: And off with those damn electric bulbs. Light a candle. I like candles.
ANDREW: The candle will have to be over there on the dresser. Ether is flammable.
HAROLD: I instructed you about ether once.
ANDREW: Indeed you did.
HAROLD: *(Mumbles.)* Níl aon tinteán mar do thinteán féin.
   (Pronounced: Neel ane tin-tawn mor duh hin-tawn fayne.)
ANDREW: There's no fireplace like your own fireplace.
HAROLD: Fine lad, you remember ... Andrew?
ANDREW: Yes.
HAROLD: Do you think I shall be able to smell my candle from far over here?
ANDREW: I do.
HAROLD: Good ... that's good ... Is it sitting in its little silver holder?
ANDREW: Aye, it tis. Mum's little silver holder.

(ANDREW lights the candle far away on the dresser and then turns off the lights.)

ANDREW: Anything else?

6

HAROLD: The candle looks like a dim orange circle. Soft edges ... Eyesight shot to hell.

(HAROLD pauses to stare at the candle, and then closes his eyes.)

HAROLD: "The Lord is my shepherd; I shall not want. He maketh me to lie down in green pastures: He leadeth me beside the still waters. He leadeth me in the paths of ..." I'm getting it out of order.
ANDREW: You are doing fine.
HAROLD: Uh ...
ANDREW: "Yea, though I—"
HAROLD: "Yea, though I walk through the valley of the shadow of death, I will fear no evil." Uh ...
ANDREW: ... "For Thou art—"
HAROLD: "For Thou art with me; Thy rod and Thy staff they comfort me. Surely goodness and mercy shall ..."
HAROLD and ANDREW together: "... follow me all the days of my life: and I will dwell in the house of the Lord forever."
HAROLD: Amen.
ANDREW: Amen.
HAROLD: I left something out ... well ... I suppose that is the way it goes. Dá fhada an lá tagann an tráthnóna. *(Pronounced: Daw aw-dah on law tog-ann an traw-no-nah.)*
ANDREW: ... Yes. The evening comes.
HAROLD: *(Pauses.)* Put out the candle.

(ANDREW walks to the candle and blows it out. The lighting remains in black. We can hear HAROLD take a deep breath in the dark.)

HAROLD: Ah. Smoke and my candle's sweet wax.

(There is a quiet pause and then we hear ANDREW'S footsteps as he walks to the bed. There is a long silent pause, and then we hear ANDREW'S footsteps as he walks to the light switch. ANDREW turns on the lights. Electric lights brighten the room. He walks to the drapes and opens them. He walks to HAROLD'S motionless body and removes the pillow and cloth from HAROLD'S face. He checks HAROLD'S pulse and then straightens HAROLD'S head and places HAROLD'S hands on his chest. He sits in the chair by HAROLD and stares at him.)

(The lights go to black.)

2. Harold's Living Room Without Bed
Months Earlier

The living room is mostly the same but without HAROLD'S bed. Books sit on the floor, chairs, and tables. HAROLD is sitting on the couch, struggling to read a book due to poor eyesight. ANDREW enters the front door, carrying dinner for HAROLD.

ANDREW: Evening Da. What are we reading tonight?
HAROLD: What am I struggling to read? These glasses have grown weaker. Damn them.

(*HAROLD tosses his glasses aside.*)

ANDREW: How does one's glasses grow weaker?
HAROLD: Much too soon you will grasp the answer to your riddle.
ANDREW: I brought dinner from Diogio's. Your favorite.
HAROLD: Spanish beans and rice.
ANDREW: Portuguese beans and rice.
HAROLD: Same thing.
ANDREW: Do not say that in front of Diogio. Where is your magnifying glass?
HAROLD: Upstairs.
ANDREW: I purchased that magnificent glass for you so you could read.

(*ANDREW unpacks dinner and sets the food on the coffee table by the couch. HAROLD climbs four steps and stops to catch his breath as ANDREW stares in silence.*)

9

ANDREW: Perhaps you should not climb steps. I shall fetch your glass.

HAROLD: Nightly, I climb these steps to sleep.

ANDREW: You know? Diogio and I visited his mother last week. She had difficulty with her staircase, breathing. Diogio hired men to move his mother's bed to the main floor. Now she does not have to—

HAROLD: *(Mumbles.)* Shoot me.

ANDREW: What did you say?

(HAROLD descends one step, stopping to take several breaths.)

HAROLD: I said, "Shoot me." Like a horse. Put me down. "Time, that aged nurse."

ANDREW: Keats.

(ANDREW attempts to take HAROLD'S hand to help him down the steps. HAROLD pulls his hand away.)

HAROLD: I can do it!

(HAROLD returns to the couch.)

ANDREW: I shall fetch your glass.

HAROLD: I do not want that ridiculously thick glass. Mr. Dickens wrote many great books. *Bleak House* is not one.

ANDREW: Hm.

(Pauses.)

Diogio showed me a new invention at his restaurant.

HAROLD: You and inventions.

ANDREW: It is called a telephone. As you talk and listen with a telephone, you are connected to people on the other side of the city who talk and listen with their telephone. The sound is clear like you are standing next to one another.

HAROLD: I do not like talking with people in my presence. Why would I talk with people on the other side of the city?

ANDREW: What should I prepare for you to drink?

HAROLD: *(Sits.)* No drink. Just the beans and rice.

(HAROLD eats and then pauses to stare at ANDREW.)

HAROLD: Are you eating or watching me eat?

ANDREW: I dinned earlier with an acquaintance at Diogio's.

Husband: A man acquaintance?

ANDREW: Uh ... a woman acquaintance.

HAROLD: Sarah is months with child, and yet you dine with a woman acquaintance?

ANDREW: Sarah and I are spending time apart.

HAROLD: Apart?

ANDREW: Time for me to think. Us both to think.

HAROLD: Monday you are certain you will marry. Tuesday uncertain. Wednesday certain. Thursday not.

ANDREW: You are in need of something to drink. Water? Tea? A small glass of wine?

HAROLD: Nothing.

ANDREW: Cup of coffee?

HAROLD: If it goes in, it comes out. If it comes out, then I have to climb those bloody stairs.

(HAROLD quietly eats and then stops.)

HAROLD: Promise me something ... As flesh and blood.

ANDREW: I shall.

HAROLD: A sworn oath upon everything you treasure.

ANDREW: What?

HAROLD: My eyes are failing.

ANDREW: Because you do not use your "ridiculously thick" eye glass.

HAROLD: This very morning, my bowels ... I did not make it to the top steps in time.

ANDREW: The bloody steps! I have apartments all over Brooklyn. One in the same building where I recently moved. Two blocks from here. Same view. All on one floor. Living room, kitchen, bedroom, water closet.

HAROLD: Your mother and I worked this house into a home. If I still had my portable chamber pot instead of that darn wash-down closet you made me install, I could take care of my business on the main floor.

ANDREW: Sweet Jesus you are stubborn. Even for an Irishman you are stubborn.

HAROLD: This home is sacred. Níl aon tinteán mar do thinteán féin.
(Pronounced: Neel ane tin-tawn mor duh hin-tawn fayne.)

ANDREW: Gaelic.

HAROLD: There's no fireplace like your own fireplace.

(ANDREW suddenly stands and paces.)

ANDREW: You're correct. This home is sacred. Like St. Patrick's Day, like Celtic Crosses, like family and church.

HAROLD: Aye. Swear to me.

ANDREW: I do not like the drift of this discussion. What are all these little stacks of books on the floor and tables and chairs?

HAROLD: I am sorting.

ANDREW: Sorting? You have these books alphabetized more accurately than the alphabet is alphabetized.

HAROLD: Books for family.

ANDREW: I am all the family you have remaining, Father.
HAROLD: Some books for you, sentimental. Some for friends. Each book has a slip of paper inside with a name.
ANDREW: It is not your time to die. Your teeth are still excellent.
HAROLD: Some of them.

(HAROLD takes a deep breath and relaxes. ANDREW paces.)

HAROLD: Sit.
(Pauses.)
Please.

(ANDREW reluctantly sits.)

HAROLD: We shall talk another day when you are calm.
ANDREW: How do I calm myself when you talk of such things?
HAROLD: Read.
ANDREW: Read?

(HAROLD hands the book to ANDREW, who sighs and opens the book.)

HAROLD: From Mr. Dickens.
ANDREW: You declared this was not a good book.
HAROLD: When you read it to me, when I hear your voice, Mr. Dickens will improve. At the marker. Top of that page.
ANDREW: *(Reads.)* "'Why, what I may think after dinner,' returns Mr. Jobling, 'is one thing, my dear Guppy, and what I may think before dinner is another thing.'" Hm.
HAROLD: *(Pauses.)* He wrote more, did he not?

DC Fidler

ANDREW: Yes.

(The lights go to black.)

3. Harold's Living Room in Early Morning Months Earlier

ANDREW enters through the front door and is yelling. HAROLD answers from upstairs.

ANDREW: Da!
HAROLD: I am upstairs.
ANDREW: Excellent news. You know Diogio?
HAROLD: One moment!

(HAROLD descends the stairs, pulling at his tie.)

HAROLD: I cannot hear you from upstairs. I tell you this every morning.
ANDREW: You know my friend Diogio?
HAROLD: I knew Diogio when he was Robert's friend Diogio.
ANDREW: I ran into Diogio out on the sidewalk. He wants to enlarge his restaurant and move to a larger space. Who has a larger space? Sullivan and I. And Diogio will immediately hire it from us! And Diogio asked that Sullivan and I import Irish Whiskey not only for his restaurant but for his friends' pubs. *Fourteen* pubs!
HAROLD: You and your Sullivan partner buy up all the spaces in New York. They will rename New York after the two of you.
ANDREW: Maybe we should buy *New Trinity Fleet Street Pen and Book Shoppe.*
HAROLD: You keep your greedy paws off of my shop.
ANDREW: Talk with Mr. Murphy. Persuade him that *New Trinity* is in too small of a space.

HAROLD: That small space has charm.
ANDREW: I have a large space with charm.
HAROLD: Large cannot have charm.
ANDREW: I am so proud of how Sullivan and I are doing.
HAROLD: You should be proud.
ANDREW: Are you proud of me?
HAROLD: I am happy for you.
ANDREW: Are you proud?
HAROLD: I am happy that you are proud that your dreams
 are being realized.
ANDREW: I disappoint you.
HAROLD: Help me with my tie. It insists on being crooked.

(ANDREW straightens HAROLD'S tie.)

ANDREW: How do I disappoint you?
HAROLD: I hoped you would seek a formal education.
ANDREW: The city teaches me.
HAROLD: I hoped you would marry, bear me
 grandchildren. I want to bounce a dozen on my knees
 before arthritis subsumes me.
ANDREW: Amazing you say that.
HAROLD: You found a wife? There is some inconceivable
 woman who will say "yes" to Andrew Carsen Cullen?
ANDREW: Sarah.

(HAROLD pulls away.)

ANDREW: We love one another, Da.
HAROLD: Sarah is your brother's wife.
ANDREW: She was my brother's wife. He died.
HAROLD: Robert is turning over in his grave hearing you
 say this.
ANDREW: Robert loved Sarah. Robert loved me. Robert
 would be pleased.

HAROLD: To say you love Sarah shows you know nothing of
Robert's heart.
ANDREW: Sarah is with child.

(HAROLD pauses and then sits.)

HAROLD: Robert's child?
ANDREW: Of course Robert's child. Robert would want me
to look after Sarah and his child.
HAROLD: You stood with me as I buried my oldest son. I
cannot understand you.
ANDREW: Father, I love Sarah.
HAROLD: And she loves you?
ANDREW: Absolutely.
HAROLD: And you ask me if I am proud.
(Stands and looks at watch.)
I shall be late for the shop.
ANDREW: Wednesday is Inventory Day. You work there
alone. No one will know you are late.

(HAROLD gets his hat.)

HAROLD: I know if I am on time or if I am late. It does not
matter if other people know or do not know.

*(HAROLD exits. ANDREW pouts. There is a knock at the
front screen door.)*

ANDREW: Come in!
SARAH: *(Enters.)* Your father was in a hurry. He tipped his
hat to me but did not wish me a good day. And now
you do not come to the door to greet me.
ANDREW: We had a quarrel.
SARAH: Not about me, I pray.
ANDREW: Well ... partially.

17

SARAH: I spoke that in jest. Why would you quarrel about me?

SARAH: I told him you are with child.

SARAH: Oh ... you did not ask me if I wanted him to know.

ANDREW: It was not my intentions to—

SARAH: I have not even told Eleanor.

ANDREW: I told Da because I want his blessing to ask for your hand in marriage.

(SARAH sits.)

ANDREW: It was a confusing dispute.

SARAH: Confusing because you and I have not discussed marriage.

ANDREW: Now you are upset with me.

SARAH: You make all these plans for my life.

ANDREW: Sarah? We love one another. We say this to one another, every day, every night.

SARAH: What will people think? It is a short time since Robert's death.

ANDREW: I can support you better than Robert. Diogio hired space from me in Manhattan and another space for a printing company on Third Avenue. We are importing Irish Whiskey for all of the—

SARAH: You are a splendid provider.

ANDREW: Am I not romantic enough?

SARAH: Sweet, gentle, strong, full of kind surprises.

ANDREW: I shall be a loving father for your and Robert's child.

SARAH: *(Pauses.)* This child is not Robert's.

ANDREW: Most certainly it is.

SARAH: He was ill for months. We did not ... lie together.

ANDREW: Months?

SARAH: *(Pauses.)* This is our child, Andrew.

ANDREW: *(Taken aback.)* How ... How can this be my child?

SARAH: The night you comforted me after Robert's death. When you and Sullivan had drunk too much of your precious "Irish."

ANDREW: You and I barely ... we just for a moment—

SARAH: A moment.

ANDREW: My child?

SARAH: Our child.

ANDREW: Then ... then this ... this is good. Our child. This is good, Sarah.

SARAH: There is something I have not told you. Something I fear to say to you. Something I fear to say to myself.

(ANDREW motions for SARAH to sit with him on the couch.)

ANDREW: There are things I think but fear to speak to anyone. It is natural.

SARAH: Robert was frightfully sick. We did not feel like husband and wife for his last days.

ANDREW: Robert never told me about this.

SARAH: It just came to be.

ANDREW: That is sad, Sarah. I did not know my brother suffered so.

SARAH: There was no happiness in Robert. No love in him.

ANDREW: His last weeks, he bossed me around. Punched me on the shoulder like big brothers do.

SARAH: Are you saying it was I?

ANDREW: No, no. You are magnificent. Glamorous. Gracious. Sensual. Robert's face brightened the instance we spoke your name.

SARAH: He did not display a bright face to me.

ANDREW: I did not know of your dejection.

SARAH: Daily it grew until one day ... Please do not judge me.

ANDREW: I could never judge you.

SARAH: Living in that house without love was unbearable. I knew that if Robert became sicker, that if he died ... I would find relief.

(SARAH turns away from ANDREW.)

SARAH: You must think me wicked.

ANDREW: It is only thoughts, Sarah. When people are tired they have desperate thoughts.

(SARAH turns to ANDREW and hugs him.)

SARAH: I was, Andrew. Tired. Confused. So much that in the end I wished Robert dead. I know it was wrong, but I wished him to die.

(ANDREW pulls away from SARAH, stands, and then walks away. He pauses.)

ANDREW: Wished him to die?

SARAH: Like you said, it was only thoughts. Silly thoughts.

ANDREW: You wished my brother to die?

SARAH: Not in the true sense of death. That would be horrid. To be back as he was before he was sick.

ANDREW: "To die?"

SARAH: The Lord Jesus took Robert. Now you and I belong to one another. And we should. We always have had desire is in our eyes when we sneaked glances across the room. Now Eleanor left you for Baltimore and Robert is not here.

ANDREW: Robert is more than not here. He is dead.

SARAH: You and I are meant to be together. This is our child, Andrew. Your child.

ANDREW: You are certain?

SARAH: Robert could not.

ANDREW: Shawn called on you after Robert's death.

SARAH: Shawn? Shawn only thinks of baseball. He is like a little brother to me. How ridiculous you sound.

ANDREW: A strong, handsome, wealthy New York Gothams' hero.

SARAH: They changed their name to the Giants.

ANDREW: Gothams, Giants. Now I see. Shawn is how you manage to buy new dress materials. Acquire that diamond necklace.

SARAH: I want you, Andrew. I always have wanted only you.

ANDREW: Robert was my brother, my friend. What did you tell Robert when he was strong and handsome? What words did you whisper in *his* ear so that he married you?

(The lights go to black.)

4. Morning in Harold's Living Room
Weeks Earlier

HAROLD is sitting in a chair and ELEANOR is sitting on the couch.

HAROLD: When you go Eleanor, I shall miss our dinner gossip of Lord Byron and Mary Shelly.
ELEANOR: Such naughty speculation.
HAROLD: Our "speculations" are invigorating.
ELEANOR: Deliciously, wickedly invigorating.
HAROLD: I have a wee present for you.

(HAROLD offers a book wrapped in cloth.)

ELEANOR: Oh Mr. Cullen! You should not have.
HAROLD: A little known mystery book. A quick read.
ELEANOR: I shall treasure this little book. Envelop every
    intriguing moment.
HAROLD: Wait until you settle comfortably on your train.
ELEANOR: By the time I reach Baltimore I shall have
    devoured it twice.
HAROLD: *(Pauses.)* Eleanor? ... I had hoped you and
    Andrew would marry.
ELEANOR: Yes ... well ... God has His plans. He takes
    Andrew and me along separate paths.
HAROLD: Indeed he does.
ELEANOR: I place my fate in the Lord's hands ... well ...
    Father will want to hear all about you, and Andrew ...
    and Robert's death, and all about *New Trinity Fleet
    Street Pen and Book Shoppe.*

HAROLD: Please tell your dear father that even after three decades, I miss him dearly. We must re-engage. Relive our youth and Dublin times, Temple Square.

ELEANOR: That will mean so very, very much to him.

HAROLD: Give your mother a fond greeting from me. I met Aideen only once. She warmed Carney's heart dearly.

ELEANOR: They do have a loving ... I shall.

HAROLD: Well ...

(HAROLD looks at his watch.)

HAROLD: I must get to *New Trinity.* Inventory day.

ELEANOR: Yes of course. I hope I have not delayed you terribly.

HAROLD: Not at all. Andrew should be along momentarily. He had a quick morning errand.

ELEANOR: I am sure.

HAROLD: He does want to see you off ... he should do at least that much ... well, have a pleasant journey. God speed you on your way.

ELEANOR: Thank you Mr. Cullen. And please do visit us in Baltimore.

HAROLD: It would do me well to get out of Brooklyn. The last time I left ... Goodness. Before Andrew was born. Back when Meara was alive and ... well ... good day.

(HAROLD gets his hat and coat, stops at the door, and stares out, speaking with his back to ELEANOR.)

HAROLD: "There is a pleasure in the pathless woods; there is a rapture on the lonely shore."

ELEANOR: "There is a society where none intrudes, by the deep sea, and music in its roar."

(With his back still to ELEANOR, HAROLD exits. ELEANOR debates whether or not to open the wrapping around the book. She peeks and there is a knock at the door. She looks around, unsure what to do. She walks to the front door but sees no one. Again she hears a knock. She walks to the dining area and looks into the kitchen and hesitantly yells.)

ELEANOR: Uh ... come in!

(SARAH enters from the kitchen.)

ELEANOR: Sarah!
SARAH: I thought you were to be on your train.
ELEANOR: A quarter past three.
SARAH: So late?
ELEANOR: I was saying farewell to Mr. Cullen.
SARAH: Of course you were. How thoughtful.
ELEANOR: You just missed him. Inventory day.
SARAH: Wednesday mornings. Yes, silly me.
ELEANOR: Yes.
SARAH: And you are sitting here alone?

(SARAH looks toward the top of the stairs.)

ELEANOR: Mr. Cullen gave me this little book. For my
    train journey.
SARAH: How nice of him. Mr. Cullen will miss you and the
    talks you two have about English and Irish literature
    and your Women's Suffrage mischief.
ELEANOR: He said as much.
SARAH: How considerate he is. And no one else is in the
    house?
ELEANOR: I just stated this minute that I am alone.
SARAH: So you did.

ELEANOR: Mr. Cullen said Andrew wished to see me off so I am waiting.

SARAH: Did he? Say that?

ELEANOR: Yes. He did. Say that.

SARAH: I suppose that is rather like Andrew. See you off. Be proper and all.

ELEANOR: We continue to be civil with one another.

SARAH: Pleasant of the two of you.

ELEANOR: Do you often enter through Mr. Cullen's back door?

SARAH: I was inspecting the nasturtiums in the backyard. I assisted Andrew and Mr. Cullen with planting the nasturtiums.

ELEANOR: It felt awkward to invite you in, it not being my house.

SARAH: Nor is it mine. Well ... I shall scurry off to the dress shop. I have new shipments of fabric from Italy. Fashion, fashion, fashion. I wish you a pleasant trip. I truly mean that.

ELEANOR: I am sure you truly mean that.

SARAH: Tell Mother and Father I do hope to visit during the holidays.

ELEANOR: I shall.

SARAH: Will you be staying with them? An extended stay?

ELEANOR: I suppose I shall stay until I settle somewhere a bit closer to the school.

SARAH: I am sure Mother and Father will be glad to have one of their daughters in the house. And it not be an extended stay.

ELEANOR: They shall be glad to have *me* there. For how ever long. They said as much.

SARAH: Our parents are polite.

(SARAH exits through the front door. ELEANOR is irritated. She sits on the couch and rapidly takes the

wrapping off of the book. She begins reading. ANDREW enters from upstairs.)

ANDREW: Sarah? Oh. Eleanor.

ELEANOR: Your father said you were out and about running morning errands.

ANDREW: Surely he heard me return.

ELEANOR: Evidently not.

ANDREW: Evidently ... uh, are you here alone?

ELEANOR: Your father was here. He left. Inventory day.

ANDREW: Ah, Wednesday morning inventory. Of course.

ELEANOR: Sarah dropped by.

ANDREW: Oh? Is she still here?

ELEANOR: She "inspected" your nasturtiums and left.

ANDREW: Nasturtiums? Right. Well then, you indeed are here alone.

ELEANOR: Your father said that you wished to see me off.

ANDREW: See you off? Yes. Of course. I wouldn't think of not seeing you off. Let me fetch my things and we can leave for the train station. Share some coffee or tea before I go to work.

ELEANOR: My train is not leaving until a quarter past three.

(ANDREW looks at his watch.)

ANDREW: Eight-fourteen.
(Pauses.)
I hope you will be content in Baltimore.

ELEANOR: In New York I help fight for women to vote. I don't know about Maryland.

ANDREW: Wyoming already granted women the right to vote. Move there.

ELEANOR: *(Awkward pause.)* I think it is more sensible if I see myself off. You have business. Rent something.

Visit your friend Sullivan. Peddle whiskey, fertilize your nasturtiums.

ANDREW: Yes, well I probably should—

ELEANOR: Your father gave me this little mystery book for the train. Such a kind, considerate man, your father. A gentleman.

ANDREW: When not at home.

ELEANOR: I am eager to begin my new book.

ANDREW: What is the book? Let me see.

ELEANOR: Good bye, Andrew.

(ELEANOR places her book in her purse and steps toward the front door.)

ANDREW: Wait. This feels unsatisfactory. We should say something ... more, something ... I am not certain what.

ELEANOR: Keats. "If poetry comes not as natural as leaves to a tree, it had better not come at all."

ANDREW: I have grown weary of poetry.

(ELEANOR exits. ANDREW stands and watches out the front door.)

(The lights go to black.)

5. Dinner in Harold's Dining Area
Weeks Earlier

HAROLD, ELEANOR ANDREW, and SARAH are completing dinner.

ANDREW: When Father would be late at work, and Grace was—

ELEANOR: Grace was your nanny?

ANDREW: Neighborly woman actually. When Grace was downstairs, Robert and I would sneak into Da's bed.

HAROLD: Into my bed incessantly. My "bed warmers."

ANDREW: Robert would blow out the candle, and then in the dark whisper to me that there was a ghost inhabiting Da's wardrobe.

HAROLD: You never told me this.
(To the women.)
He never told me this.
(To ANDREW.)
You should have told me. I would have tanned Robert's hide.

ANDREW: I did tell you. You patted him on the top of his head. Robert bemoaned that the ghost in the wardrobe was an elderly woman ghost. A ghost named Miss Havisham.

ELEANOR: As in *Great Expectations*?

ANDREW: Exactly.

HAROLD: I read the *Great Expectations* weekly serials to Robert. Always he wanted to hear the serials. Each installment repeatedly.

ANDREW: Anyway, *this* Miss Havisham, jilted at the alter like in Mr. Dickens' story, never dated. According to my big brother, she realized after her death that not dating was a grievous error. Grave.

SARAH: *(Giggling.)* Ghost. Grave.

ANDREW: Uh, yes. The ghost of Miss Havisham chose to inhabit that one, particular wardrobe.

(SARAH flirts with ANDREW.)

SARAH: Oh my, Andrew.

(ELEANOR glances at SARAH and then takes hold of ANDREW'S hand.

ANDREW: Robert terrorized me so that I buried my head beneath Da's quilts. He threatened that if that wardrobe door was not shut tightly—and in the most specific manner—Miss Havisham would slither out and feast upon young, warm, male blood.

ELEANOR: Like the penny dreadful *Varney the Vampire.*

SARAH: What is a vampire?

(ELEANOR gestures to SARAH that her question is unimportant but answers anyway.)

ELEANOR: Thomas Prest, Oren Rymer.
(Then enthusiastic.)
Go on Andrew!

ANDREW: Robert revealed to me, in his daunting, foreboding ghost voice, that Miss Havisham sucked upon her fingers while plotting to drain my blood to the last drop until my eyeballs collapsed.

ELEANOR: This is riveting!

(ELEANOR squeezes ANDREW'S hand tighter.)

ELEANOR: I had not an idea Robert Cullen could be so creative.
HAROLD: Rewriting sad Mr. Dickens.
ELEANOR: Did you know this about Robert, Sarah?
SARAH: *(Disinterested.)* No.
ELEANOR: When you two lay in bed, Robert never whispered to you of ghosts in the attic of your quaint, tiny little house's attic? Precious little house it is.

(SARAH shakes her head and becomes quiet, staring at her food.)

ANDREW: Are you all right, Sarah?
ELEANOR: She does not fancy ghosts, do you dear? *(Stands.)*
Shall we clear the dishes?
HAROLD: Do not bother with the dishes, kind Eleanor, I shall clear later.
ELEANOR: Not a bother, Mr. Cullen.

(ELEANOR clears away the dishes and yells from the kitchen.)

ELEANOR: No bother a'tall.
HAROLD: Shall we move to the living room?

(ANDREW politely helps SARAH by sliding back her chair.)

SARAH: *(Mumbles.)* Thank you.
ANDREW: Join us.
SARAH: I should help Eleanor.

(SARAH gathers dishes and exits to the kitchen. HAROLD and ANDREW move to the living room area and sit. HAROLD lights a cigar.)

HAROLD: What is it with lovely Sarah tonight?
ANDREW: Eleanor is being unusually wicked with her.
HAROLD: I observed no such thing.
ANDREW: She was—she really was.
HAROLD: Usually it is Sarah who is wicked with Eleanor.
ANDREW: Well ... "I observed no such thing."
HAROLD: Careful. It is Eleanor who sleeps at your side.
ANDREW: Father! Eleanor and I do not sleep—
HAROLD: A father knows certain things. "That purple-laced palace of sweet sin."
ANDREW: You may know Keats, but you do not know many things you think you know about me.
HAROLD: I know what I know ... Look me straight in the eye.
ANDREW: *(Avoiding eye contact.)* I shall do no such thing.
HAROLD: Straight in the eye ... Uh huh, even as a boy you could not look me in the eye and lie.
ANDREW: Eleanor has never been one to ... shall we say, be open with her affections.
HAROLD: And yet many a night you do not return home.

(Suddenly there is sound of a dish breaking in the kitchen.)

ANDREW: *(Yells.)* Is all fine in there?
ELEANOR: *(Yells from off stage.)* We are fine! Carry on!
HAROLD: She is waiting for a tad more commitment. She certainly played with your hand at the table tonight. No encouragement from you.
ANDREW: Eleanor has a talent of hand playing at public tables when everyone is watching.

HAROLD: Do you give that poetic lady your heart?

(ANDREW looks down in shame. ELEANOR enters the dining area and observes the men, remaining unnoticed.)

HAROLD: Even as a lad, you shielded your heart from women folk. So different from your brother. Robert lost your mother when he was old enough to have her in his heart. You lost your mum when you were ... younger.
ANDREW: Blasted theories about nonsense.

(ELEANOR partially enters the living room area.)

ELEANOR: Is this a men-only gathering?
HAROLD: It should not be. Join us, my dear. Lighten our spirits.
ELEANOR: I shall, thank you.

(ELEANOR fully enters the living room area and sits.)

HAROLD: Ask your sister to join us.
ELEANOR: Sarah, I think, is still mourning. She is washing dishes in there as if to scrub away two years of marriage.
HAROLD: "Scrub away?"
ELEANOR: With enough violence to shatter a piece of lovely Haviland China.
HAROLD: *(Pauses.)* When I lost my Meara, I did not "scrub away." I cherished.
ANDREW: Devoutly and restrictively enough you never dated again.
HAROLD: I spoke vows from my heart. There was no need to look further.

ANDREW: Perhaps Sarah wishes to move on. Find another.
HAROLD: Robert has been dead only three weeks. How
dare you speak of such a thing.
ELEANOR: Did Sarah say she wished to move on?
ANDREW: Not with words. I surmise from your description
of her "scrubbing away Robert" that perhaps she—

(HAROLD abruptly stands.)

HAROLD: No one scrubs away my Robert.

(HAROLD walks toward the stairs.)

HAROLD: I shall retire early. Read a passage or two from
your brother Robert's Dickens' serials and erase this
disagreeable conversation.

(ELEANOR and ANDREW stand.)

ELEANOR: Mr. Cullen? I hope I did not offend.
ANDREW: Nor I, Father.

(HAROLD turns to ELEANOR and ANDREW.)

HAROLD: One day, if you two finally marry, have children
of your own, you will know what it is to have that bond
of parent to child. Know sacred flavors of that bond.
ANDREW: "Flavors?"
HAROLD: "Flavors" is rather poetic. Eleanor?
ELEANOR: Why yes. "Flavors" is poetic, Mr. Cullen.
HAROLD: Indeed.
(He climbs a few stairs and turns.)
Even after death that bond persists. It warms one's
soul.

(He exits up the stairs.)

ELEANOR: I feel foolish.
ANDREW: Da will be fine.
ELEANOR: Well ... I should go. Are you coming?
ANDREW: I shall linger a bit. Assure Da is settled.
ELEANOR: Yes of course you will.

(ELEANOR kisses ANDREW on the cheek. ANDREW does not return the kiss or even seem to notice.)

ELEANOR: It is still light outside. My favorite time of day.
Dusk. Were I an artist.
(Sighs.)
I feel perfectly safe walking home alone.
ANDREW: Are you suggesting I walk you home?
ELEANOR: When has my walking two blocks concerned
you?

(ANDREW demonstrates no response.)

ELEANOR: That was such a delightful, delightful dinner.

(ELEANOR exits. ANDREW sits in silence, thinking deeply. SARAH enters and begins to gather more dishes. Coming out of his daze, ANDREW stands.)

ANDREW: Sarah. Leave those. Please. Come here.

(SARAH approaches.)

ANDREW: I apologize for Eleanor's rudeness this evening.

(SARAH grabs ANDREW and kisses him passionately on the lips. ANDREW passionately kisses back for a moment. SARAH pulls away.)

SARAH: I am sorry. I do not know what overcame me.
ANDREW: Uh ... you are missing my brother, missing your husband Robert, I suppose.
SARAH: I should go.
ANDREW: Stay.

(ANDREW takes SARAH'S hand.)

SARAH: No.

(SARAH pulls her hand away and gathers her belongings.)

ANDREW: Do you wish for me to walk you home?
SARAH: What would people say?
ANDREW: It would be my pleasure.

(SARAH gives ANDREW a quick kiss on the lips and then places her finger on ANDREW'S lips as if to keep him quiet. SARAH exits. ANDREW walks to door and stares after SARAH.

(The lights go to black.)

6. Harold's Living Room in Early Evening
Three Weeks Earlier

HAROLD is putting on his coat and hat when there is a knock on the door. HAROLD opens the door.

HAROLD: Robert, Sarah. I was just leaving to visit the McCoys. William is not well. Come in, come in.

(ROBERT and SARAH enter.)

ROBERT: We were strolling through the neighborhood. Is Andrew home?

HAROLD: He is on his way with Sullivan to Coogan's Pub. Hurry and you can catch them.

ROBERT: No. Actually, we came to see you.

HAROLD: Oh. Come in. I can visit William at a later moment. Can I get you something? Tea?

ROBERT: No, thank you. We cannot stay long.
(He sits.)
Sarah? On second thought, go into the kitchen and make us some tea.

HAROLD: I just had my tea.

ROBERT: Well ... I would like a cup.

(He gestures to SARAH who then goes to the kitchen.)

HAROLD: You do not look well.

ROBERT: I have been laboring long hours.

(ROBERT searches for the candy dish.)

ROBERT: Where is the candy dish?

HAROLD: I no longer purchase candy. You eat too much of it.
ROBERT: I am fit ... anyway, with Sarah in the kitchen, we can have a man-to-man, father-son talk.
HAROLD: We could.
ROBERT: I am hoping.
HAROLD: Ah! That is why you sent Sarah to the kitchen.
ROBERT: Pops, I came here to—
HAROLD: Pops! You have not called me "Pops" in years.
ROBERT: Da ... this is embarrassing. Please pull off your coat. Sit.

(HAROLD sighs, pulls off his coat and sits.)

HAROLD: So serious.
ROBERT: I have come to ask you for a favor ... I am having a wee bit of financial problems and ... we cannot afford rent this month.
HAROLD: Both of you are working.
ROBERT: We are.
HAROLD: And you don't have money? My God!
ROBERT: I owe a wee bit to the bank.
HAROLD: Money for rent and your bank?
ROBERT: I shall pay you back next month. Business is improving. Boats arrive every day from Ireland and Italy.
HAROLD: I walked past your butcher shop last week. I did not see one customer.
ROBERT: Some days are slow, specific times of the day.
HAROLD: I must have walked by on a slow day at a specific time.
ROBERT: This is not easy to ask you.
HAROLD: Did you ask Andrew? He has more money than all of us. More than all the neighborhood.
ROBERT: I am embarrassed enough.

HAROLD: Your brother is generous.
ROBERT: He is younger, looks up to me.
HAROLD: Ask him.
ROBERT: Please ... Do not make me beg you.
HAROLD: I sell books. I make a living, not a rich living, but a living. I have a little money saved. Not much.
ROBERT: What ever you can spare will help.
HAROLD: Did you add up what you need, for your month of rent, for your bank?

(ROBERT reaches into his pocket and retrieves a crumpled piece of paper. HAROLD studies it.)

HAROLD: How can this amount be so?
ROBERT: I did not tell Sarah. We have not had rent money for six months.
HAROLD: You said one month. Now six months.
(Sighs.)
Tomorrow? Meet me at *New Trinity* at lunchtime. We shall visit my bank together.
(Pause.)
Ní thagann ciall roimh aois.
(Pronounced: Nee hog-ann kee-al riv eesh)
ROBERT: You know I do not speak Gaelic.
HAROLD: "Sense does not come before age."

(ROBERT nods but remains silent.)

HAROLD: *(After a pause.)* I should visit William now.
ROBERT: Thank you, Da.

(HAROLD stands. ROBERT follows, hugs Harold, backs away, and nods with gratitude.)

HAROLD: Tell your lovely wife I found it necessary to visit William.

(HAROLD exits. ROBERT walks to the kitchen door.)

ROBERT: He is gone.
SARAH: *(Enters.)* Will he give us the money?

(ROBERT nods and SARAH hugs him.)

SARAH: I told you he would.
ROBERT: That was the most difficult thing I have ever done.
SARAH: Your father is more than happy to help you. His duty.
ROBERT: Da works in a book shop. He does not earn much. A little savings.
SARAH: We shall pay him back.
ROBERT: We spend far too much for your dress design materials.
SARAH: My dress designs will bring large amounts of money some day.
ROBERT: You do not sell dresses. You wear the dresses yourself.
SARAH: That is not true.
ROBERT: That is true.
SARAH: I must wear dresses so other people see them. People compliment them. It is how I let people know I am capable of designing.

(ROBERT sighs and does not look well. He pulls out a small dark-colored glass bottle and drinks a sip. He sits.)

SARAH: Robert?

(ROBERT rubs his forehead and eyes and then his left side.)

SARAH: Robert? Are you all right?
ROBERT: My left side hurts. This medicine will help.

(SARAH bends down to better see ROBERT.)

SARAH: Did you eat something, drink something before you left the house?
ROBERT: I was worrying about what to say to Da.
SARAH: Dr. Kaufman said you must eat and drink when you feel weak or something dreadfully serious will happen.

(ROBERT begins trembling.)

ROBERT: Bring my sugar water.
SARAH: You never listen to Dr. Kaufman. Every time we see him, he tells you what to do. Writes it on notes for you.
ROBERT: Please get my water.
SARAH: You are stubborn and do not listen to anyone.
ROBERT: *(Weaker.)* Please?
SARAH: Fine. I shall make sugar water.

(SARAH exits to the kitchen. ROBERT wipes sweat from his forehead with his handkerchief. He trembles much more. He winces and holds his left side. He sips more from his small bottle. He tries to stand but is weak and kneels on the floor beside the chair, holding the chair, having labored breathing.

ROBERT: *(Yells.)* Sarah!

SARAH: *(Off stage.)* Patience!

(ROBERT turns so he is sitting on the floor beside a chair. He becomes restless. SARAH enters carrying a glass of cloudy water.)

SARAH: Here is your precious sugar water.

(SARAH walks toward ROBERT and stops.)

ROBERT: Thank God.

(ROBERT holds out his hand for the glass. SARAH stands frozen, staring at ROBERT, holding the glass out in front of her.)

ROBERT: *(Faint.)* Sarah? Give me the glass.

(SARAH continues to stare. She takes a step back.)

ROBERT: Why are you waiting?

(SARAH continues to stare and then slowly lowers the glass and places it on a table.)

ROBERT: *(Disbelief but with little energy.)* I need ...

(SARAH stands motionless, staring at ROBERT.)

ROBERT: I must have—

(ROBERT begins to twitch and slides lower onto the floor. He begins to have larger convulsions. SARAH remains motionless as she watches ROBERT. ROBERT becomes still except to let out one deep exhale. SARAH

watches for a moment and then sits on the couch. She stares at ROBERT's motionless body. Finally, she turns away her gaze.)

(The lights go to black.)

INTERMISSION

7. Harold's Living Room in Morning
One Year Earlier – 1885

ROBERT and ANDREW are sitting as ANDREW sips a glass of
Irish Whiskey with a whiskey canter sitting next to him.
ROBERT, a bit dizzy, unfolds a cloth and shows the
contents.

ROBERT: Dr. Kaufman gave these to me. The yellow seeds
   are lupine. This little bitter thing is zedoary seed, all
   the way from the Orient. And this bottle is extract
   from fenugreek.
ANDREW: Fenu what?
ROBERT: An Indian, Hindu remedy.

   (ROBERT eats a piece of candy from the candy dish.)

ANDREW: And Dr. Kaufman believes you to have diabetes?
ROBERT: You are not listening. Dr. Kaufman said I do *not*
   have diabetes. I have sweet tasting urine only some of
   the time.
ANDREW: He drank your urine?
ROBERT: I did not ask.
ANDREW: That is disgusting.
ROBERT: Sometimes I have spells of feeling dizzy, weak.
   Other times I have pain on my left side, here.

   (ROBERT points to his left side just below his heart.)

ANDREW: Your heart?
ROBERT: *Not* my heart. It is mighty like an ox.
ANDREW: How strong is the pain?
ROBERT: Dr. Kaufman made an opium mixture for me.

ANDREW: Opium? Good Lord, Robert.

ROBERT: Stop exaggerating this or we are finished talking. I simply have to eat when I feel weak, sip my solution when there is pain.

(ROBERT eats a second piece of candy.)

ANDREW: *(Mumbles).* Making allowance for candy.

ROBERT: *(Yells.)* Sarah! Hurry with my extract and sugar water!

ANDREW: Can these strange seeds or opium kill you?

ROBERT: Dr. Kaufman is treating a famous, wealthy man for similar side pain and up-and-down sugar levels. Thanks to him the man is perfectly well, however, he won't tell me the man's name. I'd kill to know.

(SARAH enters with a glass of cloudy water.)

ANDREW: Sullivan's older cousin has diabetes and it destroyed his sexual capabilities.

ROBERT: I don't have diabetes! And I assure you your big brother is highly virile, fertile.
(To SARAH.)
Right delicate sweetheart? Always on top of my game.

(ROBERT forces a laugh. SARAH gives a polite but not agreeing smile, making no eye contact.)

SARAH: I shall leave you two conquerors of women to discuss your manhood.

ANDREW: Robert's boasting bores me. Please stay.

ROBERT: Someone has to instruct you, little brother.

(ROBERT drinks the water.)

ANDREW: That looks and smells terrible.
ROBERT: That it tis.
SARAH: Where is Eleanor this morning?
ROBERT: Yes, where is your fair fiancé?
ANDREW: I imagine she is sleeping after her strenuous day. I doubt she shall appear "fair." "Unsettled" is more typical.

(ELEANOR speaks through the front door screen.)

ELEANOR: I am veritably "settled," thank you. Good morning everyone.
(She enters.)
I had a perfectly splendid excursion to a magnificent literary conference at Columbia University yesterday. I took a horse car across the Brooklyn Bridge and beyond, and then the Ninth Avenue El up to Columbia and back again.
SARAH: My gracious. How did you survive those deafening loud steam engines and dreadfully smelly horses doing their business?
ANDREW: Eleanor exercises her "independence," no matter the smell.
ELEANOR: "Independence" for women is to be admired, not admonished, Master Andrew Carson Cullen.
ANDREW: Master? I am a boy in her eyes.
ELEANOR: Perpetually.

(ELEANOR quickly kisses ANDREW on his cheek.)

ELEANOR: We had a reading of works by a stimulating, invigorating Irish author. Mr. Oscar Wilde.
SARAH: Never heard of him.
ELEANOR: Deliciously controversial. The scandal of Dublin literary circles. British, too.

SARAH: Mr. Wilde should come to the Washington Heights Polo Grounds, appear at a baseball game. Then people would know of him.

ELEANOR: Mr. Wilde would be dismayed to learn he has no baseball fame. Andrew? Mr. Wilde made an appearance here in '82. A colleague gave me an autographed note from that appearance. A gift for you.

(ELEANOR hands a note to ANDREW who sarcastically holds it to his chest.)

ANDREW: I shall frame this note and place it in my rental office for all to see.

(ELEANOR snatches the note.)

ELEANOR: I shall give it to your father.

(ANDREW holds his hand over his heart as he recites poetry.)

ANDREW: "Self-love forever creeps out, like a snake, to sting anything which happens to stumble upon it."

SARAH: Mr. Wilde wrote that?

ELEANOR: Lord Byron wrote that. Andrew magically recalls Lord Byron whenever he wishes to taunt me. Is that a new dress, Sarah? Quite smart.

SARAH: This is the same design as last month but I added this Valenciennes Lace around the waist. Valenciennes Lace is being revived in the great Parisian House of Drecoll. This season many French gowns are aglow with it. I am re-introducing it to New York.

ELEANOR: Lovely. Andrew darling? You could purchase one of Sarah's "revived" Parisian-laced dresses for me. I wage that Sarah will render you a thrifty price.

ANDREW: I shall pay full price. Consider it my contribution to New York's literary circles.

SARAH: Oh. I only had enough lace for this one creation, but I can order more.

ELEANOR: How disappointing. I require the dress for next week.

ROBERT: I am certain Sarah will alter this one for you.

ELEANOR: I would not dream of stealing Sarah's sentimental ensemble. Andrew will take me shopping. *(To ANDREW.)* You are accompanying me next week to Monsieur Le Platt's gallery showing? Yes? Maybe? Getting cold feet? Forgot? Hm?

ANDREW: Eleanor reminds me with endless lavender notes stuffed into my pockets. I cannot forget no matter how much I strive.

ELEANOR: You refer to me in third person, even though I am present. How distant. In any event, success. Well then ...

(ELEANOR places the note on a table.)

ELEANOR: Make certain your father finds this note. Robert? Will you be a dear and ask Andrew for me if he will walk me home?

ROBERT: Uh ... I need to discuss financial arrangements with Andrew.

ELEANOR: A butcher shop and a real estate developer? I cannot imagine. Sarah? Do stroll with me.

SARAH: Uh ... I was hoping to talk Robert into escorting me to a baseball game.

ROBERT: I cannot accompany you today.

ELEANOR: Are the New York Gothams playing?
SARAH: Oh yes! One o'clock!
ELEANOR: Your recent description of the players intrigues me. Allow me to escort you.
SARAH: Really?
ROBERT: Two women? Unescorted?
ELEANOR: Do not be a stick in the mud, Robert. It is perfectly safe, fashionable these days for women to have outings.
ROBERT: Sarah only attends so she can watch the players. One Shawn chap specifically.
ELEANOR: What interest is a game if one is not rooting for someone specifically? Shawn is the handsome chap?
SARAH: They are all equally handsome ... from the distance I keep.
ELEANOR: Oh? I thought you had met him in person. My mistake.
SARAH: Oh, Robert? Please?
ROBERT: You two must be home before dark.
ELEANOR: Come, Sarah. First we shall amble by your house. Andrew will spring for a private carriage to the game, won't you dear?
SARAH: Thank you, Andrew. Thank you, Robert.

(SARAH kisses ROBERT on his lips for several seconds until finally ELEANOR clears her throat.)

ELEANOR: We should hurry, baby sister.
SARAH: Oh thank you, thank you. This is so exciting. I have been dying to introduce you to the Gothams. I mean to baseball. It will be grand not to have our bothersome men distracting us.

(ELEANOR and SARAH laugh and energetically exit together. ANDREW sits.)

ROBERT: I do not trust them together.

ANDREW: Any stray man approaching those two Irish ladies should fear for his life. About what "financial" arrangements were you referring?

ROBERT: I have been thinking of setting up my own restaurant. A small place, here in Brooklyn, nothing grand like what Diogio is developing in Manhattan.

ANDREW: And you have money to establish a restaurant? I thought you were struggling.

ROBERT: Well ... I am. And Sarah's business struggles. She has not sold a dress in two months.

ANDREW: Then how can you launch a restaurant?

ROBERT: I want to partner with you.

ANDREW: Partner a restaurant? I know nothing of your culinary arts.

ROBERT: I have expertise. You have capitol.

ANDREW: You have been out of restaurant work and back at being a butcher for a year.

ROBERT: I know everything about restaurants and Diogio is willing to guide me. Look how successful he is.

ANDREW: Ask him to be your partner.

ROBERT: He is not willing.

ANDREW: I see.

(ANDREW stands and paces. He pauses to think before speaking.)

ANDREW: Do you remember what you once told me growing up? When I asked you to lend me a quarter?

ROBERT: A quarter?

ANDREW: We were paperboys. You told me "no." You said, "It is business." On second thought, I shall run and meet up with our women for that Gotham's game. You should rest. You look weak.

(ANDREW exits. ROBERT continues sitting and finishes drinking his water. He stands and pours himself a drink of whiskey from a decanter.)

(The lights go to black.)

8. Dinner at Harold's
One Year Earlier — 1884

HAROLD, ROBERT*, ANDREW, ELEANOR, and SARAH are*
completing dinner in the dining area and talk as they
walk to the living room area and sit. HAROLD stands,
clinks his glass with his spoon, and offers a toast.

HAROLD: It is heartwarming to have family gathered. My
   daughter-in-law Sarah, my daughter-in-law-to-be
   Eleanor.
ROBERT: I foresee a very long engagement for these two.
SARAH: Robert!
HAROLD: And to my two sons. I wish Meara were here to
   share in this splendid moment. To the memory of my
   lovely wife Meara. To the hopes and dreams for a
   blessed future for our family.
ROBERT: and ANDREW: Here, here.

(All toast their crystal glasses and drink. HAROLD
sits.)

ANDREW: You exceeded my dining dreams, old brother.
ELEANOR: The most divine roasted pheasant I have tasted.
   Succulent bacon and mushroom garnish.
ROBERT: I presented that exact dish for the chef at
   Churchill's.
SARAH: His response, "Robert is destined for a big career."
ROBERT: "Accomplished career."
SARAH: "Accomplished career."
ELEANOR: You attended our promising chef's delectable
   presentation?

SARAH: I did indeed. And then he whisked me off to
Tiffany's.

ELEANOR: Tiffany's?

ROBERT: *The* Tiffany's. Down on Broadway.

SARAH: We got to view the Audubon flatware. And are you
ready? We viewed the Tiffany diamond.

ROBERT: *The* Tiffany diamond. 128 carats. One day I shall
buy my little bride a colossal Tiffany wedding band to
replace this small temporary one.

SARAH: *(Protective.)* I like this band, Robert. It is
sentimental—but I would allow you to buy me a small
diamond-studded bracelet.

ROBERT: Now that is my queen.

(ROBERT kisses SARAH.)

ELEANOR: Mr. Cullen? What book are you burying your
head into these days?

HAROLD: Henry Ellis' *Original letters, Illustrative of
English History.*

ROBERT: Exactly what I read in my spare time.

ANDREW: When did you last read a book?

ROBERT: Probably the same day you did.

ANDREW: I read a book weekly, thank you very much.

ELEANOR: Tell us Mr. Cullen. What are you learning?

HAROLD: When Catherine of Aragon's first husband,
Arthur, the Prince of Wales died, she was encouraged
to marry her husband's younger brother Henry, who
became King Henry the Eighth.

ELEANOR: Catherine married her younger brother-in-law?

HAROLD: Through much of history it has been the duty of
younger brothers to marry their deceased older
brothers' wives. Provide the widows with children.
That way, the lineage continues.

ANDREW: Surely that was the exception.

HAROLD: Julius Caesar unearthed the fact that it was customary amongst ancient Britons for brothers, sometimes fathers and sons, to have wives in common.

ANDREW: My God those Brits!

HAROLD: And Greeks, Romans, our own ancient Celtic culture.

ANDREW: Thank God they civilized.

HAROLD: When I was a lad, in the village of Clodalkin, ten kilometers west of Dublin, a family's oldest son died. The younger son's wife, feeling saddened for her sister-in-law, demanded that her husband lie with her widowed sister-in-law, impregnate her sister-in-law with child to keep her company. The village supported this arrangement. So I am told.

ANDREW: Preposterous.

(To ROBERT.)

Is that not ludicrous?

HAROLD: Read your Bible, Andrew. Deuteronomy. "If brethren dwell together, and one of them die, and have no child, the wife of the dead shall not marry without unto a stranger; her husband's brother shall go in unto her, and take her to him to wife, and perform the duty of an husband's brother unto her."

ANDREW: Why on earth would you commit such a damnable verse to memory?

ELEANOR: Intriguing. Don't you think, Sarah?

ANDREW: Most unholy.

HAROLD: Read your Genesis. God slain Onan for refusing to carry out such duties.

ANDREW: No child should be permitted near a Bible.

ELEANOR: Be careful around your dangerous restaurant knives, Robert. If something were to happen to you, gracious knows, I may demand Andrew perform husbandly duties with Sarah.

(ELEANOR laughs.)

ROBERT: That is not amusing.
SARAH: She is jesting, my dear.
ROBERT: It is ill-considered humor.
SARAH: Your father brought it up.
HAROLD: And that is what I am reading.
ELEANOR: I did ask. Thank you.
ROBERT: Well, Sarah would immediately learn that my
    brother has little passion.
ANDREW: Did you insult my manhood?
ELEANOR: Older brothers must not know how hot the
    blood of younger brothers stir.
ANDREW: Eleanor! Decency forbids.
ROBERT: Tell us, Eleanor, how hot stirs young Andrew's
    blood?
SARAH: All of you are making me blush.

(SARAH hides her face.)

SARAH: I fancy your tiny residence to be much like a
    schoolmarm's library or a nun's convent.
ROBERT: Oh, when you dare make Sarah blush, watch out!
ELEANOR: I inhabit a small flat now, dear, because—
ROBERT: "Flat?" Suddenly we sound so French.
ELEANOR: The Brits say, "flat" as well now. In a small *flat*
    because you tossed me into the gutter in order to live
    with your butcher-restaurant husband in that
    charming little house that you and I once shared.

(ROBERT places his arm around SARAH.)

HAROLD: Well, this is quite spirited.
ROBERT: We deeply thank you, gracious Eleanor. Now let
    us conclude this topic before dueling pistols are pulled.

ELEANOR: Duels must be fanatical fun.

(ROBERT kisses Sarah.)

ROBERT: I have an idea. I shall treat the four of us to a baseball game tomorrow.

SARAH: Baseball?

ROBERT: You have never been to a baseball game.

SARAH: Baseball appears ... lifeless.

ROBERT: What about it Andrew? Introduce my wife and your fiancé to a bit of sport?

ELEANOR: I have papers to grade this weekend.

ROBERT: Schoolmarm.

ANDREW: I promised Sullivan I would look at "a flat" tomorrow.

ROBERT: Good Lord. Are you moving into "a flat" with Sullivan? The two of you do spend an inordinate amount of time together.

SARAH: You do stay over at Sullivan's often enough.

ANDREW: I stay at Sullivan's when and only when we have had a bit much.

ROBERT: Drowned in your kegs of "Irish." One day you will grow out of that.

ANDREW: Our company is purchasing that flat to lease.

ROBERT: No profit in leasing.

ANDREW: On Canal Street.

ROBERT: In Manhattan? That is prime real estate.
(To SARAH.)
Well then my bride, just you and I for baseball tomorrow.

(SARAH frowns as if she smells a foul odor.)

SARAH: Baseball.

ROBERT: Diogio introduced me to three Gotham players. If you behave, I shall introduce you to those spirited, wild men.

SARAH: Tomorrow I had plans to shop for material for my new pattern.

ROBERT: Along the way, we can stop and purchase your material. And then I shall dazzle your eyes and senses with a house tour.

SARAH: A house tour? Tell me.

ROBERT: I laid down the first month's rent.

SARAH: A large house?

ROBERT: I am going to be a famous chef. You and I must live accordingly.

SARAH: Oh my, oh my. I am feverish with excitement.

(SARAH kisses ROBERT passionately.)

ROBERT: Excitement? Perhaps we should continue this discussion at home.

SARAH: What shall I wear tomorrow?

ROBERT: You are stunning every day.

SARAH: If we are to tour a grand house and visit Diogio's men friends, I must be more stunning.

ROBERT: Please excuse us, Father.
(Standing.)
I am afraid we are leaving you with a disordered kitchen.

HAROLD: Be off children. Enjoy your cricket game.

ROBERT: Baseball, Pops. Baseball.

HAROLD: *(Mumbles.)* Pops.

SARAH: Good day Mr. Cullen, Andrew, Eleanor.

(ELEANOR and HAROLD stand to say good bye. ROBERT starts to leave, but then returns to grab a piece of candy and hurriedly eats it.)

ROBERT: And two candies for the road. Or three.

(ROBERT and SARAH laugh as they exit.)

ELEANOR: Baseball. Well ... to grade some papers.

(She gathers her belongings.)

ANDREW: We should attend a game sometime.
ELEANOR: If I can keep my mind from idling by bringing along a rough draft of *The Woman's Bible*. Ms. Susan Anthony is delivering a lecture about her hope for an International Council of Women.
ANDREW: Let me walk you home.
ELEANOR: Why of course, gentleman Andrew.
ANDREW: Or should I help you with the kitchen, Father?
HAROLD: No, no, I am fine.
ELEANOR: Your father is kindly lying. Stay and assist.
ANDREW: But he said—
ELEANOR: Stay and assist him.
ANDREW: I shall drop by later to assure you are fine.
ELEANOR: We shall see, shall we not?

(ELEANOR gives ANDREW a kiss on the cheek, and then gives a lady-gentleman handshake to HAROLD.)

ELEANOR: Mr. Cullen. As always, I had a delightful time being mentored by you. I very much would enjoy discussing your fascinating cultural, religious, dark ideas again, should you spare me the time.
HAROLD: I am honored to spare time for you anytime, dear Eleanor.
ELEANOR: Gentlemen.

(She exits.)

HAROLD: You should have escorted her. Then returned to help me.

ANDREW: I cannot win.

HAROLD: She is a strong woman.

ANDREW: Worse now that she in involved with this Woman Suffrage Association.

HAROLD: She is bold.

ANDREW: She perpetually tests my resolve. Why can't she behave more ... normalized?

HAROLD: Like Sarah?

ANDREW: You read too much Bible. I shall hide it from you. To the kitchen?

HAROLD: *(Chuckling.)* To the kitchen.

(ANDREW and HAROLD carry dishes as they exit to the kitchen.)

(The lights go to black.)

9. Late Afternoon in Harold's Living Room
One Year Earlier – 1883

HAROLD is introducing ELEANOR and SARAH to ROBERT and ANDREW.

HAROLD: Robert? Andrew? This is Ms. Eleanor Fianna Walsh.
ELEANOR: Pleased to make your acquaintance.
HAROLD: And Ms. Elizabeth Sarah Walsh.
SARAH: Please call me Sarah. An honor to make your acquaintance.
HAROLD: And my sons. Robert Scott.
ROBERT: Delightfully splendid to meet you. Both of you.
HAROLD: And Andrew Carson.
ANDREW: Ladies.
HAROLD: Please have a seat. I was a boyhood friend of Eleanor and Sarah's father, Carney. Back in Dublin.
ROBERT: So you told us.
ANDREW: Repeatedly.
HAROLD: May I bring you ladies some tea?
ELEANOR: That would be lovely. Oh, here is the little Byron book I borrowed. "To mingle with the universe and feel—"
HAROLD: "What I can ne'er express, yet cannot all conceal."

(HAROLD and ELEANOR laugh with pleasure.)

ANDREW: "And a voice less loud, thro' its joys and fears, than the two hearts beating each to each."
HAROLD: Andrew Carson Cullen! That is not Byron.
ELEANOR: Robert Browning, but very nice, Andrew.

HAROLD: Please excuse me ladies, gentlemen, the tea.

(HAROLD exits to the kitchen. ELEANOR, SARAH, ROBERT, and ANDREW sit.)

ROBERT: Well ... uh ... father told us about meeting both of you at *New Trinity Fleet Street Shoppe.*
ELEANOR: Mysterious and intriguing establishment. Calming.

(ROBERT speaks to ELEANOR.)

ROBERT: And you are the fashion designer?
ELEANOR: I am the teacher.
SARAH: I am the fashion designer.
ROBERT: I should have known. Your lovely dress ... oh ...
(To ELEANOR.)
Not that your dress is not lovely, too, naturally.
ELEANOR: Naturally.
ANDREW: What do you teach?
ELEANOR: Elementary pupils. Literature. Irish and British literature.
ANDREW: Father told us he enjoys discussions with you about Irish writers.
ELEANOR: A bit about the Irish ... mostly we discuss Lord Byron.
ANDREW: "But what is hope? Nothing but the paint on the face of existence."
ELEANOR: Impressive, Andrew Carson.
ANDREW: Although as boys, Father read all things Irish to us.
ELEANOR: And did you enjoy all things Irish, Robert Scott?
ROBERT: I hardly know my Byron from my Keats from my Browning.
ANDREW: Those poets are each and every one British.

ROBERT: My point precisely.
(Chuckles with embarrassment.)
At least I recognize poets' names.
SARAH: That is as much as I know, too, Robert.
ELEANOR: Sarah does know the works of Parisian fashion
houses.
ROBERT: Fashion?
SARAH: I do. There is Jacquettes de Maison Boistay, and
Mademoiselle Marguerite, then Maison Edmond
Paget, Melanie Percheron, yes and Mademoiselle
Delansorne, and of course Fashion House Laborde,
and—
ELEANOR: Quite remarkable, Sarah—She would go on for
days.
ANDREW: Quite rousing.

(SARAH giggles with embarrassment.)

SARAH: Goodness. I want to "invent," so to speak, my own
fashion house here in New York.
ANDREW: For upscale clientele. I can tell.
SARAH: Is it that obvious? Oh absolutely. And why not?
ROBERT: I wish to cater to an upscale clientele as well, but
satisfying their culinary palates.
SARAH: A cook!
ROBERT: A chef.
SARAH: Pardon me. I meant to say, "chef." How clumsy of
me.
ROBERT: Perhaps one day you well-fashioned ladies will
dine upon my delectable cuisine.

*(SARAH giggles and whispers into ROBERT's ear.
ROBERT laughs loudly.)*

ROBERT: Absolutely yes.

(ROBERT's laughter slowly subsides as he tries to regain composure. Once he does ANDREW speaks.)

ANDREW: Robert works in a butcher shop.

SARAH: Oh?

ROBERT: It is a temporary station while I prepare to apprentice with fine chefs at Delmonico's.

ANDREW: Is that not the restaurant where a drunken man recently fired a shot into the restaurant as he screamed that he wished to put a scare into rich people?

ELEANOR: I read that. Class warfare. I fear it is an overture of what is to follow.

ROBERT: Different Delmonico. On the other hand, I may one day cook for the great New York restaurateur, Louis Sherry. Who knows? The Waldorf Astoria, Churchill's, Maxim's. With so many fine possibilities it is difficult for me to choose.

SARAH: I know what you mean. You are a butcher now, but you will climb your ladder of destiny. I do not usually reveal this, but temporarily?

(Quieter voice.)

I am a seamstress.

ELEANOR: In a sweat shop.

SARAH: What was that, Eleanor?

ELEANOR: Your fashion house, one day, will be the talk of New York.

SARAH: My ladder of destiny.

ROBERT: Andrew, what "ladder of destiny" do you fancy?

ANDREW: Oh, uh ... I am inclined toward business. Dull.

ELEANOR: Any business specifically?

ANDREW: Uh ... investments, speculations.

ROBERT: Andrew is still charting his direction.

SARAH: Do not fret Andrew. You will find your ladder. A few months ago, I did not know at all that I would one day design dresses. I only wanted to marry into wealth. And one day, just like that, snap, I saw a refined lady step from her carriage in Baltimore.

ELEANOR: And you settled upon marrying wealth.

SARAH: Not at'tall. The fine lady's dress, although fashioned from impressive materials, lacked an artist's eye. I wanted so badly to rescue that pitiful woman. So Andrew, do not fret. Walking down the street your calling will grab you.

ANDREW: I am eager to be grabbed.

SARAH: The three of us striving toward our dream careers. How exciting.

ELEANOR: Am I not also striving?

SARAH: You are firmly situated as an elementary school literal teacher.

ELEANOR: Literature teacher. So are you saying that I have no need or desire to dream and grow?

(SARAH shrugs.)

ELEANOR: My young sister. All people dream and grow. Literature instructs us thus. Does it not, Andrew?

ANDREW: Uh ... I suppose.

ELEANOR: Prose and poems of successes and tragedies. Both possibilities inform us. What a charming, nurturing house. Did you young men grow up here?

ROBERT: We did. Andrew and I and our Father.

SARAH: And your mother?

ELEANOR: Sarah!

ROBERT: It is fine, Sarah. Our mother died with the birth of Andrew.

SARAH: How sad for you, Andrew.

(ANDREW is stunned for the moment. He tries to speak but cannot.)

ROBERT: Allow me to show you ladies the remainder of the house.
SARAH: And Andrew. The two of you.

(HAROLD enters carrying a formal tea.)

HAROLD: And tea is served.
ROBERT: Actually, Da conducts the best excursions. He has a story for each and every book and artifact.
ELEANOR: How positively charming, Mr. Cullen. After all, it is stories about one's belongings that enchant.
HAROLD: Why yes it is, Ms. Walsh. Indeed.
ELEANOR: Eleanor, please.
HAROLD: Eleanor. This way ladies.

(HAROLD walks toward the stairs and SARAH follows.)

SARAH: I so like the fabric of these draperies. Perhaps a bit of lace would help.
HAROLD: We shall begin with the upper floor and work our way down.
SARAH: And this tiny carpet. So ... Oriental.
HAROLD: I believe it is Ukrainian. Left to me by a kind elderly woman at St. Francis.

(HAROLD, ELEANOR and SARAH begin exiting up the stairs. HAROLD turns to ROBERT and ANDREW.)

HAROLD: Are you boys coming along?
ROBERT: I have taken this tour. St. Francis rug and all. But Andrew would enjoy a tour.

(ANDREW laughs and shakes his head "no.")

HAROLD: Very well, boys. Ladies? I have you to myself.

(HAROLD, ELEANOR, and SARAH exit up the stairs.)

ROBERT: I like Sarah.
ANDREW: So do I.
ROBERT: Eleanor is very much a snob.
ANDREW: Like all older brothers and sisters.
ROBERT: Sarah is full of life. Feisty.
ANDREW: Eleanor is closer to your age. Sarah is closer to
    mine.

*(ROBERT hurries up the stairs, skipping a few steps,
speaking as he exits.)*

ROBERT: Sarah? I shall join you after all.

*(ANDREW sighs, shakes his head, and then slowly walks
up the stairs.)*

(The lights go to black.)

10. Morning in Harold's Living Room
Days Earlier

ROBERT enters through the front door. ANDREW is sitting on the couch in his bed robe, reading his newspaper as ROBERT talks.

ROBERT: Is Da here?
ANDREW: Upstairs eternally shaping his moustache.
ROBERT: I have someone I want you to meet. My best friend.
ANDREW: I already know Casey.
ROBERT: My new best friend. Diogio.
ANDREW: What happened to Casey?
ROBERT: Casey is in love. Never available.
ANDREW: Diogio? Italian?
ROBERT: Portuguese. I know you two will become good friends.
ANDREW: Not Irish?
ROBERT: We are permitted to have non-Irish friends.
ANDREW: Sullivan, Finn, Davin, Cillian—
ROBERT: We live in New York. Branch out.

(ANDREW continues reading the newspaper.)

ANDREW: As you wish, big brother.
ROBERT: Diogio is an impressive chef.
ANDREW: I don't need a friend to cook for me.
ROBERT: You are as stubborn as our father.
HAROLD: *(Yells from off stage.)* I heard that.

(He descends the stairs as ROBERT eats candy from the candy dish.)

ROBERT: The two of you only associate with Irish blokes.
HAROLD: And you eat far too much candy.
ROBERT: You place the candy in the bowl. I eat it.
HAROLD: Andrew does not. I do not.

(ROBERT speaks to ANDREW.)

ROBERT: Why do you not eat candy?
ANDREW: It makes me feel bloated, unwell.
ROBERT: Da?
HAROLD: I shall live forever, so I do not eat candy that I may keep my teeth forever.
ROBERT: If you do not want me to eat candy, do not place it in the bowl.
HAROLD: Your mother declared candy in a dish to be "festively decorative."
ROBERT: One more piece and I'll stop.

(He eats another piece of candy.)

HAROLD: Did you interview for the position at the library?
ROBERT: I do not have a love affair with books like you and Andrew.
HAROLD: It was a guaranteed job. Guaranteed decent pay.
ROBERT: I interviewed with Mr. Brandini.
HAROLD: The butcher shop?
ROBERT: Yes.
HAROLD: He is Italian.
ROBERT: He is American. Like Andrew. Like me. Born here in America.
HAROLD: So, you are ashamed your father is Irish.
ROBERT: You left Ireland.
HAROLD: *(To ANDREW.)* Talk with your brother. I do not wish to.

ANDREW: I am American, still, Robert will not listen to me.

HAROLD: You two torture me. Andrew? Did you submit your college application?

ROBERT: I wager "no."

HAROLD: Is he correct? That is an essential piece of paper for your life.

(ANDREW shrugs.)

HAROLD: Why did your mother and I leave Ireland? So one day our children would have fine educations.

(ANDREW stands and walks toward the stairs.)

HAROLD: Before you run upstairs and pout, I have news. Two sisters, the ages of you two, visited *New Trinity*. Although they are from Baltimore, their parents are from Dublin. Their father, Carney, was my best friend in grade school and then again when we were old enough to down a pint or two in Temple Square.

ROBERT: Or three, or five, or eight pints.

HAROLD: Kilbeggan Irish whiskey. We were young and foolish lads. Less foolish than you two.

ANDREW: May I be excused? I have plans with Sullivan. I need to dress.

HAROLD: I invited these two charming ladies to dine with us Saturday evening.

ROBERT: On Saturday, I am expected by Casey and his girlfriend to go to the Gotham game. If she allows Casey to go.

HAROLD: I require both of you to attend this dinner and I require both of you to be gentlemen. Understood?

ANDREW and ROBERT: Yes, sir.

HAROLD: Now you are excused to go pout.

(ANDREW exits up the stairs. HAROLD sits.)

HAROLD: A butcher shop.
ROBERT: It is temporary, Da, until I gain position as an apprentice at Delmonico's.

(ROBERT eats more candy. HAROLD sits.)

HAROLD: Cooking.
ROBERT: An honorable chef position.
HAROLD: "Chefing" food we common folk cannot afford. As your mother and I and you set sail for America—Andrew kicking the walls of her belly—she had dreams for you.
ROBERT: Mum would be proud for me to become a chef.
HAROLD: Meara loved books and learning.
ROBERT: I remember her.
HAROLD: Do you? Age two?
ROBERT: A wee bit.
HAROLD: What?
ROBERT: Her voice reading, soft … her funeral with snow.
HAROLD: All day long snow. Meara was never sick a day in her life. Before that snow.

(ROBERT nods with great focus. HAROLD pauses and talks in a secretive tone.)

HAROLD: You cannot tell this to anyone, certainly not to your brother.

(ROBERT remains quiet, but remains intense.)

HAROLD: Do I have your word?
ROBERT: Aye.

HAROLD: Your mother ... died as she gave birth to Andrew. *(Pauses.)* A fine, strong pregnancy, all the way through. She took one look at baby Andrew and instantly we all witnessed Meara love Andrew deeply ... she smiled at him ... peacefully closed her eyes. A wee bit of rest. She was gone.

(HAROLD pauses and then stands and walks up the stairs.)

(The lights go to black.)

11. Harold's Living Room Near Dusk
Six Months Earlier — 1883

The room has the dim light of dusk and low light from two candles, one in the center of the room and one near the wall. HAROLD enters from the kitchen, carrying a small canister. He fetches his reading glasses and sits next to the candle in the middle of the room, mumbling as he reads from the side of the canister.

HAROLD: Na‑na‑na‑na‑na‑na.
(Pauses.)
"Avoid open flame." Oh dear God.

(He quickly sets down the canister and hurriedly blows out the candle. He wets his fingers with saliva and touches the wick to assure it has no live ember. He examines the wick as if he is a scientist scrutinizing a new bug species.)

HAROLD: Out.

(He sighs and picks up the canister and walks to the door to have light to read and prepare his materials. He puts on his glasses and reads, and then exits to the kitchen. He returns with a small cloth. He carefully opens the canister, holding it a straight‑arm distance from his face. He takes a deep breath and holds it as he pours a small amount of liquid onto the cloth. He drops the cloth into a small pan and then closes the canister. He runs a few feet away and finally takes a loud, deep breath.)

HAROLD: Dear God, grant me strength.

(He looks back at the pan.)

HAROLD: And fresh air. In your name.

(He hurries to open the front door. He inhales several, exaggerated deep breaths.)

HAROLD: Thank you for fresh air, Lord Jesus.

(He leaves the front door open and retrieves the pan and cloth and carries them with him as he exits to the kitchen. There is a pause and then HAROLD enters and looks around the room and grabs a small ragged couch pillow. He exits with the pillow to the kitchen. There is a pause. Harold enters and collapses into half sitting, half lying on the couch. He takes several deep breaths and relaxes. ANDREW enters through the front door, carrying a small slatted wooden box with its contents wrapped in a cloth.)

ANDREW: Cold air is rushing in. Are you airing out the house?
HAROLD: That I am.
ANDREW: I brought something to show you.

(ROBERT runs down the stairs into the living room and grabs his hat and coat.)

ROBERT: It is dark and cold down here.
ANDREW: Robert! I have something to show you!
ROBERT: I am terribly late. One of Casey's friends made an appointment for me to prepare dinner for his uncle,

one of the assistant chefs at Maxim's. This is my chance. One day—

(ROBERT holds up his hands as if he is pointing at a marquis he is reading.)

ROBERT: "Chef Roberto." Then "Café Roberto."
ANDREW: Well "Roberto" Cullen, you happen to be Irish.
ROBERT: Italian or French sounds better. Upper crust. I'll bring leftovers.
HAROLD: Hm. Café Roberto.

(ROBERT kisses HAROLD on the top of his head and then grabs a piece of candy from the candy bowl and eats it.)

ROBERT: One day, no more left overs. You'll dine with white Belfast linen. Irish Waterford crystal. A grand piano and fireplace. Women hanging from both of our arms, aye little brother?

(ROBERT pulls ANDREW to him and tries to kiss him on the top of his head, but Andrew pushes him away)

ANDREW: I'll find my own woman, "Roberto."

(ANDREW laughs and shakes his head. ROBERT hurriedly exits.)

ANDREW: Well, I genuinely did not care to show this to Robert. Just you, Pops.
HAROLD: "Pops." Another American vulgarism.

(ANDREW sees the canister near the door and looks closely at it.)

ANDREW: What is this?
HAROLD: One canister of ether.

(ANDREW lifts the canister.)

HAROLD: Do not touch that! That little canister can create
    an inferno and snatch your last breath before you can
    blink.
ANDREW: An admirable addition to our home.
HAROLD: Aye. When it is called for.
ANDREW: And what need have you for this, this—
HAROLD: Vile, villainous, perplexing substance?
ANDREW: Not an ingredient for one of Robert's cooking
    disasters I pray. Or is this poison from one of your Mr.
    Shakespeare's plots?
HAROLD: Mr. William had no access to the likes of this
    toxicant I promise ya.
ANDREW: Father dear? Why does one require the likes of
    meether?
HAROLD: Ether.
ANDREW: Ether.
HAROLD: Ah. The little kitty has gone to its maker.
ANDREW: The runt? The sick one?
HAROLD: Aye she has.
ANDREW: You poisoned one of our kittens?
HAROLD: She took its last wee breath peacefully. All with
    no bit of suffering. Three paws already with God, only
    one paw barely touching our earth. I gave her a bit of
    a nudge into God's sweet, merciful hands.
ANDREW: You murdered her!
HAROLD: I did no such thing.

*(ANDREW hurriedly exits to the kitchen, pauses, and
slowly enters carrying the pillow.)*

ANDREW: And smothered her with this pillow?

HAROLD: Eased her into a gentle sleep. God choose not to wake her.

ANDREW: She would have died soon enough.

HAROLD: Soiling its wee self and lying in its own spit, its little ribs aching from so little air.

ANDREW: God decides when.

HAROLD: God decided today that I would be his instrument.

ANDREW: Do we sit in the same church?

HAROLD: Same pew. Sunday after Sunday.

ANDREW: We must not be hearing the same words.

HAROLD: God is merciful.

ANDREW: Merciful? Today God was shaped into what form was convenient for *you.*

HAROLD: Your mother drowned many a runt kitten and puppy what took ill.

ANDREW: Mum did?

(HAROLD nods.)

ANDREW: Well, drowning is ... is more natural.

HAROLD: Aye that it tis. Cannot argue you that one ... well maybe I could.

ANDREW: I know you could.

(ANDREW removes a crank machine and light bulb from the crate.)

HAROLD: Dá fhada an lá tagann an tráthnóna.
   (Pronounced: Daw aw-dah on law tog-ann an traw-no-nah.)

ANDREW: And that would translate?

HAROLD: No matter how long the day, the evening comes.

75

ANDREW: Now that it is darker, I can demonstrate this for you.

(ANDREW closes the front door and holds a match to the candle in the middle of the room. HAROLD abruptly stands.)

HAROLD: *(Yells.)* No flame close to the ether! Great God Almighty!

(HAROLD grabs the canister and carries it to the kitchen. He re-enters, closing the door firmly behind him.)

HAROLD: Next time, maybe only the pillow. It is peaceful enough without risking I torch all our sentiments. A pillow. Like with Desdemona when she—
ANDREW: *Othello.* I know, I know.

(ANDREW lights the candle in the middle of the room.

ANDREW: Now, allow me to show this to you. An invention not created for death. Electricity.
HAROLD: I know about electricity. I read *Frankenstein: The Modern Prometheus.* Full of death.
ANDREW: *Frankenstein* is fiction.
HAROLD: I know what is fiction and what is science. Do not lecture me on—
ANDREW: Pops! I borrowed this just for tonight. I have to return it in the morning. Sit.
HAROLD: Sit?
ANDREW: You will not believe this.
HAROLD: I do not believe you ordered your own father to "sit." And called me, "Pops."
ANDREW: Da? Please?

HAROLD: All right, all right.

(HAROLD sits.)

HAROLD: I am obeying as you ordered your own "Pops" to "sit."
ANDREW: Now watch this.

(ANDREW turns the crank and the bulb lights. He pauses to look at HAROLD'S face. The bulb slowly dims. HAROLD sits motionless. ANDREW pauses.)

ANDREW: Well?
HAROLD: Well what?
ANDREW: What do you think?
HAROLD: It is a magic trick?
ANDREW: It is science.
HAROLD: Science.
ANDREW: It may appear to be a table-top trick to you Da, but one day, take my word, homes, businesses will all have these. Wealthy households already have electric lights.
HAROLD: First wealthy homes had gas lamps. Then all homes and businesses. Now it will be "electricity." Everyone turning little cranks.
ANDREW: Not turning hand cranks. Wires bringing in the electricity, like pipes bring in gas. But with switches. You walk into a room, turn a switch and voila. The room instantly lights. Bright light. No flame. Light you can use to read your beautiful books.

(ANDREW walks to the wall and blows out the candle near the wall. He returns to the crank box and bulb and sits.)

HAROLD: My lovely books.

(ANDREW begins cranking the box and the bulb brightens.)

ANDREW: Put out that other candle.
HAROLD: This candle rests in the little silver holder your mother brought over on the clipper. Meara's little silver holder. I like this candle.
ANDREW: I know you like it. We have the last house in Brooklyn without gas lights.
HAROLD: When it is time for my day to end, I put out my candle. I smell smoke and sweet scents of melting wax.
ANDREW: Please?
HAROLD: All right, all right.

(HAROLD blows out the last candle and the room goes black except for the bulb.)

HAROLD: Ah. Smells.

(ANDREW turns the crank faster and the bulb lights brighter.)

ANDREW: There. Brighter light.

(HAROLD is delighted and animated as he looks around the room.)

HAROLD: It is bright.
ANDREW: See that switch? While I crank, you move the switch.
HAROLD: This?
ANDREW: Yes. A switch.
HAROLD: I shall.

(HAROLD flips the switch and the bulb immediately goes to total black as does the room.

(Soft finale music begins beneath the scene.)

(ANDREW continues cranking.)

ANDREW: Dark.
HAROLD: Very dark.
ANDREW: Now move the switch again.

(HAROLD clicks the switch and immediately the bulb and room light.)

ANDREW: Light.
HAROLD: A fine, strong light. I *could* read by this light.
    Possibly without my glasses.
ANDREW: Again.

(HAROLD clicks the switch and the room darkens.)

ANDREW: Dark.

(HAROLD clicks the switch and the room lights.)

ANDREW: Light.

(HAROLD clicks the switch and the room darkens. There is a pause. HAROLD clicks the switch and the room lights. He looks around in delight.)

HAROLD: Well, will you look at that.

(HAROLD smiles at ANDREW. He clicks the switch and the room darkens. There is a pause. HAROLD clicks the switch and the room lights. He pauses. HAROLD clicks the switch and the room darkens. ANDREW pauses and then quits cranking. HAROLD and ANDREW both sit quietly in the dark. There is silence except for the soft music. After a moment in the dark, HAROLD speaks.)

HAROLD: Dá fhada an lá tagann an tráthnóna.
(Pronounced: Daw aw-dah on law tog-ann an traw-no-nah.)
ANDREW: No matter how long the day, the evening comes.
HAROLD: Aye. Tis true.

(A spotlight rises on ANDREW sitting on the footstool at the front of the stage, dressed with the same hat and sweater that he wore in the beginning of the play.)

ANDREW: Tonight, like other nights this month, I visit Da's house. I sit here on his footstool ... his books and assorted fragments of art. I work to hold it ... to shine light upon it.

(ANDREW remains motionless as music continues, and then speaks.)

ANDREW: And it begins.
HAROLD: *(Yells from the dark.)* No! On the end table!
ANDREW: Ah. Yes. The book. Miss Wilshire.

(The music rises in volume. After a moment the spotlight dims to black.)

FINALE

About the Author

A native of the South, DC Fidler has combined a career in academic psychiatry and cultural psychiatry with a lifetime of playwriting, acting, directing, composing music, and teaching creative writing and the dramatic arts.

He studied theatre, writing, chemistry, medicine, and psychiatry at the University of North Carolina at Chapel Hill, where he served on the faculty. He later served on the faculty at West Virginia University, teaching cultural psychiatry, clinical psychiatry, and acting.

A licensed psychiatrist, DC Fidler has lived and worked with the Alutiiq tribe in Akhiok, Alaska; the Al Moqbali Bedouin tribe near Sohar, Oman; the Kalkadoon Aboriginal Tribe in the outback of Queensland, Australia; and the Te Tau Ihu Maori Tribes on the South Island of New Zealand.

He began his acting career in outdoor dramas, summer stock theatre, and local films and television at age ten. He has written scripts and composed music for over fifty medical educational videos at UNC-CH and WVU. He has written twenty plays that have been produced in various community theatres and universities across North Carolina, Virginia, and West Virginia, as well as St. Louis, Sacramento, San Diego, Los Angeles, Boston, Chicago, and New York City.

He consulted and appeared in educational productions for HBO, ABC, and PBS and performed in numerous stage plays including: *Hope is the Thing with Feathers, Night of January 16th, Thieves' Carnival, Blood Wedding, Our Town, A Life in the Theatre,* and *Fool for Love.*

Presently, he is a scriptwriter, film director, and medical consultant for educational films using professional actors to demonstrate mental health issues. In addition, he is an active member of the Dramatists Guild of America and the Charlotte Writers' Club.

Fidler previously chaired the Video Committee for the American Psychiatric Association and served as President of the Association for Academic Psychiatry. In 2003, he was inducted as a Fellow of the Royal College of Physicians of Ireland. He serves on the Arts and Humanities Committee for the Group for the Advancement of Psychiatry where he is co-producing a video series on the History of Psychiatry.

He is author of the textbook, *Psychiatry for Actors: Using Psychiatric Principles to Build Characters,* and author of the novel, *Boogieban.*

Musicals by DC Fidler
- Pied Piper (With Lauren Horacek)
- Healer Man
- Medicine Show

Plays by DC Fidler
- Voices in the Woods
- Guilt by Association (With RJ Casey)
- Three Diaries
- Master William Bowlinggreen and Company
- Shiraz
- The Anniversary of Miss Nanette Pringle
- School Children Hiding Under Desks
- Grams
- Camp Uni
- Boogieban (Two-Actor Version)
- Boogieban (Seven-Actor Version)
- Ahulaqs
- Elk and Wolf (With Travis Teffner)
- Santee Delta (With Travis Teffner)
- Celtic Crossing
- Stone Touchin'
- Daugherty Park Merry-Go-Round
- La Dynastie
- Gyges Solution
- Begat

Short Plays by DC Fidler
- Persons
- Cruise
- Mobile to Where
- Oman Truce
- Second Amendment
- The Greek God Club
- Four X
- Microscopic Misconceptions
- Drone Guns
- Moon Bugs (With Travis Teffner)

Novels and Textbooks by DC Fidler
- Boogieban
- Psychiatry for Actors: Building a Character Using Psychiatric Principles